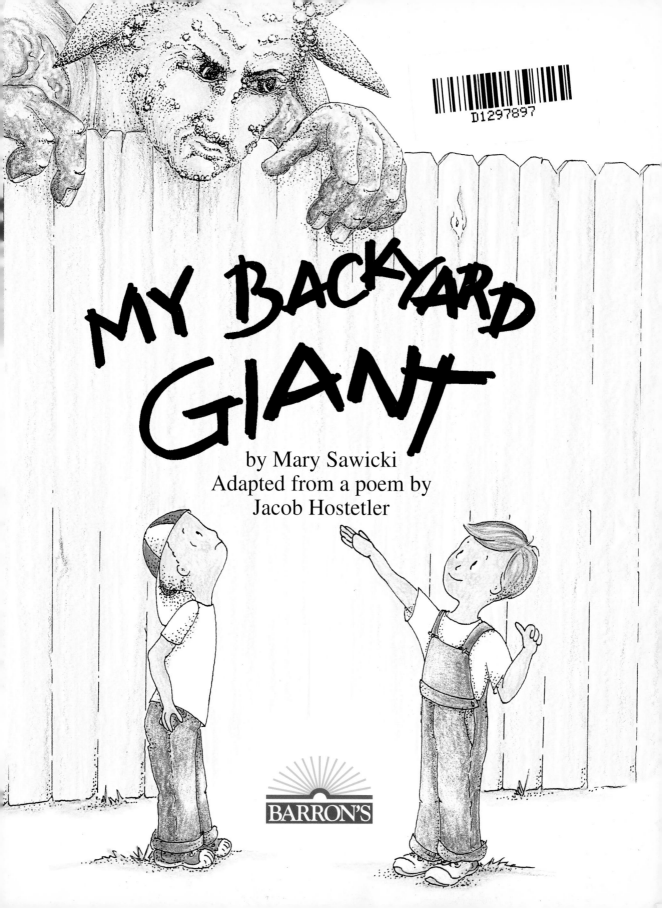

MY BACKYARD GIANT

by Mary Sawicki
Adapted from a poem by
Jacob Hostetler

BARRON'S

Dedication
For Genevieve and Al Sawicki
who many years ago gave me a backyard giant
to stand under in the rain.

And thanks to
Jacob, Jesse, and Karl for the poem,
the posing, and the love.

Published by Barron's Educational Series, Inc.

All inquiries should be addressed to:
Barron's Educational Series, Inc.
250 Wireless Boulevard
Hauppauge, NY 11788

International Standard Book No. 0-8120-1736-6 (P)   0-8120-6399-6 (H)
Library of Congress Catalog Card No. 93-29762

Library of Congress Cataloging-in-Publication Data

Sawicki, Mary
    My backyard giant / by Mary Sawicki; adapted from a poem by Jacob Hostetler.
    p.   cm.
    Summary: A boy describes his "backyard giant" to a friend who
imagines something mean and scary until he discovers its true identity.
    ISBN 0-8120-1736-6 (P)   0-8120-6399-6 (H)
    [1. Sunflowers—Fiction. 2. Imagination—Fiction.]
I. Hostetler, Jacob. II. Title.
PZ7.S2674My   1994
[E]—dc20
                                                        93-29762
                                                        CIP
                                                        AC
PRINTED IN HONG KONG
3456 9955 987654321

"Did you say a GIANT! . . . a real giant, not pretend, an actual giant lives in your backyard?"

"Yep."

"What does he look like?"

"Well . . . let's see . . . he has a BIG, yellow, bumpy face, with pointy things sticking out all over his head."

"Pointy things?"

"Yep."

"And he's taller than my
privacy fence."

"He has really big arms. They're rough
and green."

"And he has one, long, strong, skinny leg."

"Aren't you afraid to go in your backyard?"

"Afraid? Oh no. He's a very nice giant."

"He lets the birds sit on his head. And squirrels climb all over him."

"He doesn't mind? . . . the squirrels I mean?"

"Tickles him I expect."

"He's so nice that one day when it started to rain, I stood real close to him and he kept me dry with his big, green arms."

"Is he back there right now? . . . the giant?"

"Nope. Now that summer is over it's too cold for him out back. I took him into my room to keep him warm."

"In your room?"

"Yep, in my room. He didn't want to come in. I had to drag him. He really was stubborn too. You know how stubborn giants can be, don't you? Well, he dug his toes into the ground and I really had to pull hard to get him to move."

"Boy, my mom sure would be mad at me if I dragged
a yellow-faced, green-armed, one-legged giant into
my room!"

"My mom wasn't thrilled either but when I told her
about the time he kept me dry in the rain . . . well she
softened up a bit."

"So, he's in your room right now? The giant is in your room?"

"Yep."

"Could I . . . could I see him?"

"Sure, follow me."

"That's your giant? Your yellow-faced, green-armed, one-legged, bigger than your privacy fence giant? That's a SUNFLOWER!"

"Sure is. What did you expect?"